EXOTIC PETS
OPEN

EXIT
THE HIPPOPOTAMUS IS OUT BACK

 • LIBRARY OF CONGRESS CONTROL NUMBER: 2010906971
SCHOLASTIC, NEW YORK, NY 10012 • PRINTED IN SINGAPORE 46 • DESIGNED BY DAVID SAYLOR • FIRST EDITION, 2011

When I bought my rhinoceros, I didn't really know what I was getting into.

He was a nice animal. Quiet, shy.
He stayed in the yard. Kept to himself.

After a couple of days, I noticed that my rhinoceros wouldn't chase a ball.

Or a stick.

Or a frisbee.

He didn't roll over.
He didn't do anything.

I called a rhinoceros expert.
"Does he yank on his leash?" she asked.
"No," I said.
"Does he attack other rhinoceroses?"
"No," I said.
"Does he poop on the rug?"
"No!" I said.

"So what's the problem?"

"He doesn't do *anything*," I said.

"Actually," she said, "rhinoceroses only do two things. Pop balloons and poke holes in kites."

I couldn't believe it. Pop balloons and poke holes in kites?! How pathetic.

And then I thought: What if we went to the park and there was a man selling balloons?

Luckily, nothing happened.

But what if somebody was flying a kite?

Lots of kids were flying kites.
But nothing happened.
My rhinoceros didn't pop balloons!
He didn't even poke holes in kites!

I began to wonder about my rhinoceros.

Maybe he was a clunker. Maybe I should have bought a hippopotamus instead.

On the way home from the park, I saw a robbery! One of the robbers was getting away in a balloon, the other was escaping in a kite.

The robber in the balloon was taunting the crowd.

I looked at my rhinoceros and pointed to the balloon. "Pop!" I said.

To my surprise, my rhinoceros leapt into the air. He swooped at the balloon with his tusk.

POP! went the balloon and down fell the robber.

I looked up at my rhinoceros and pointed to the robber in the kite. “Poke a hole!” I yelled.

My rhinoceros swooped over and poked a big hole in the kite.

Down fell the robber.

Everybody was amazed by my rhinoceros.

The police chief raced up to me. "Is this your rhinoceros?"

"Yes," I said.

"Well, you've got a really special one. He can pop balloons and poke holes in kites!"

"I know," I said. "And guess what else?"

“He can fly, too!”

POLICE

I don't think I'll buy a hippopotamus.